# Parzival

✦ ✦ ✦

## THE QUEST OF THE
## GRAIL KNIGHT

# Parzival
### ◆ ◆ ◆
# The Quest of the Grail Knight

RETOLD BY

# KATHERINE PATERSON

LODESTAR BOOKS

Dutton ◆ New York

No character in this book is intended to represent any actual person; all the incidents of the story are entirely fictional in nature.

*Library of Congress Cataloging-in-Publication Data*

Paterson, Katherine.
Parzival: the quest of the Grail Knight / retold by
Katherine Paterson.
p.   cm.
Summary: A retelling of the Arthurian legend in which Parzival,
unaware of his noble birth, comes of age through his quest
for the Holy Grail.
ISBN 0-525-67579-5 (alk. paper)
1. Perceval (Legendary character)—Legends.   2. Arthur, King—
Legends.   3. Arthurian romances. [1. Perceval (Legendary
character)—Legends.   2. Arthur, King—Legends.   3. Knights and
knighthood—Folklore.   4. Grail—Folklore.] I. Wolfram von
Eschenbach, 12th cent. Parzival.   II. Title.
        PZ8.1.P2316Par   1998
    398.22—dc21   97-23891   CIP   AC

Published in the United States by Lodestar Books,
an affiliate of Dutton Children's Books,
a member of Penguin Putnam Inc.,
375 Hudson Street, New York, New York 10014

Published simultaneously in Canada
by McClelland & Stewart, Toronto

*Editor:* Virginia Buckley   *Designer:* Claire B. Counihan

Printed in the U.S.A.
First Edition

1   3   5   7   9   10   8   6   4   2

for
CHRISTOPHER FRANCESCHELLI
with
admiration, gratitude,
and affection

# Contents

# The People

**ANFORTAS**  The Grail King of Wild Mountain. In legend, Anfortas is also called the Fisher King or the Angler. He is Parzival's uncle, brother to Queen Herzoloyde. His other sisters are Sigune's dead mother, Schoysiane, and Repanse de Schoye, who is the Grail Bearer. Anfortas's brother is Trevrizent, the hermit.

**ARTHUR**  Legendary king of Britain, head of the Knights of the Round Table, located at his court in the town of Camelot. He was the son of Uther Pendragon and Igrain, who was said to have fairy blood.

**CLAMIDE**  King of Iserterre and Condwiramurs's unwelcome suitor.

**CONDWIRAMURS**  Queen of Brobarz, which she inherited from her father. She is niece to Gurnemanz and a cousin of Parzival's cousin, Sigune. She becomes Parzival's wife.

**CUNDRIE THE SORCERESS** Although physically repugnant, she is in truth a prophetess and the messenger of the Grail.

**CUNNEWARE** Sister to Parzival's sworn enemies through his mother.

**FEIREFIZ** Parzival's half brother, son of Gahmuret by the queen of Zazamanc, whom Wolfram describes as a "dusky Moorish queen."

**GAWAIN** Son of King Lot of Norway, he is a nephew of Arthur. He is also a distant relative of Parzival's. In all the legends surrounding him, Gawain epitomizes the best of knighthood.

**GUENEVER** Variously spelled. She is Arthur's wife and thus queen of Britain.

**GURNEMANZ** The prince who is Parzival's mentor. He is the father of Liaze, whom Parzival rashly promises to marry, and the uncle of Condwiramurs. All three of his sons have died, one in defending Condwiramurs.

**HERZOLOYDE** Sister to Anfortas, the Grail King; Trevrizent, the hermit; Repanse de Schoye, the Grail Bearer; and Schoysiane, who died giving birth to Sigune. Herzoloyde inherited the kingdoms of Waleis and Norgals, lands that were added to her husband Gahmuret's when they married. In this story, she is best known as Parzival's mother and Gahmuret's sorrowing widow.

**ITHER**  Also known as the Red Knight. He is a distant relative of Parzival's and quite a ladies' man. After Parzival kills Ither, Parzival becomes known as the Red Knight because he has put on Ither's armor and is riding his sorrel, or reddish-colored horse.

**IWANET**  A young page in King Arthur's court who befriends Parzival. He is a kinsman of Queen Guenever.

**JESCHUTE**  Wife of Herzoloyde's sworn enemy, Duke Orilus.

**KARDEIZ**  Twin son of Parzival and Condwiramurs, brother to Lohengrin. He inherits the secular kingdoms of Brobarz from his mother and Anjou, Waleis, and Norgals from his father.

**KAY**  King Arthur's seneschal (counselor or chief steward). He is Arthur's foster brother and so has a lot of influence in court, although his temper and cruelty make him an unpopular figure.

**KINGRUM**   Seneschal of King Clamide.

**LAHELIN**   Brother of Orilus and Cunneware. With his brother, Orilus, he has conquered the kingdoms of Herzoloyde, namely Waleis and Norgals, and is thus her sworn enemy.

**LIAZE**   Daughter of Gurnemanz. She is Parzival's first crush, soon forgotten after he meets her cousin, Condwiramurs.

**LOHENGRIN**   Twin son of Parzival and Condwiramurs, brother to Kardeiz. He inherits the throne at Wild Mountain.

**ORILUS**   Enemy of Herzoloyde, brother of Lahelin and Cunneware, and husband of Jeschute, the duchess from whom Parzival takes the ring and brooch.

**PARZIVAL**   Variously spelled Parsifal, Percival. In Wolfram's romantic poem, he was the son of Gahmuret and Queen Herzoloyde. In English tradition, Percival is the son of Pellinore. In later English texts, Galahad replaces him as the Grail Knight.

**REPANSE DE SCHOYE**  Parzival's maternal aunt and the Grail Bearer. Repanse later marries Parzival's half brother, Feirefiz.

**SEGRAMORS**  A member of Arthur's court and a cousin to Queen Guenever.

**SIGUNE**  Parzival's first cousin, daughter of Schoysiane, Herzoloyde's sister. Her knight has been killed by Duke Orilus.

**TREVRIZENT**  The hermit. He is maternal uncle to Parzival and brother of Anfortas, the Grail King. He is also uncle to Sigune.

# Parzival

• • •

## THE QUEST OF THE
## GRAIL KNIGHT

# One
### The Boy

**N** the ancient days, when Arthur was king of Britain, there lived a boy who had never heard of the great son of Pendragon or of his bold knights. The only home the boy had ever known was a cottage in the wilderness of Soltane, and the only parent he had ever known was his mother. He was never called by his proper name; indeed, he didn't even know that he had one. The plowmen who worked his mother's fields and the drovers who tended her flocks called him Young Master. His mother called him her Dear Boy. Strangers rarely came

into the district, but when one happened by and asked his name, he would say, "You may call me Young Master or Dear Boy or whatever you please."

He was a happy child. He loved the forests where the birds sang, the streams where the fish jumped, and the fields where the golden grain danced. He did not desire the pomp of King Arthur's court because he had never dreamed it existed. He did not long for learning because he had never seen a book. And he never feared death because he had yet to hear of Heaven or Hell.

He spent his days exploring the forest, fishing the streams, and making toys for his own amusement. When he was a little boy, he was content to devise whistles from reeds and construct watermills for the stream. But as he grew older, he came to idolize the huntsmen who brought rabbit and pheasant and venison for his mother's table, so he carved for himself a bow from yew wood and sharpened sticks from the oak tree, to which he fastened feathers from the henyard.

One day, crossing his mother's fields, he came upon a flock of larks pecking seeds from the plowed ground. One bird rose high into the air, singing a song so beautiful that it pierced the boy's heart. Without thinking, he raised his bow and shot his arrow into the sky. The song ceased mid-note, and the singer dropped like a stone to the earth.

When he saw that his arrow had killed the bird, the boy cried out and broke his crude bow over his knee. Indeed, for many days, whenever he heard the song of a lark, he burst into tears, remembering his thoughtless act.

His mother was distraught. She could not bear for her child to be unhappy. She ordered her peasants to capture all the larks that came into her fields and wring their necks, so her son would not weep.

But this only made the boy more unhappy still. "Why do you kill the little birds?" he asked his mother. "They've done nothing wrong."

His mother relented. Kissing his hair, she said softly, "Who am I to go against God? It is his will that the birds should sing for happiness."

"Who is God, Mother?" the boy asked. For his mother, thinking to leave her past unhappy life behind, had never told him of the Creator.

"Why, Dear Boy, God is he who is King of Heaven. He has made the world and in his love took human form to save it. You must pray to him and ask his help." And, realizing how she had failed to instruct him in things of the spirit, she went on to warn him. "There is another who is the lord of Hell. He is called the devil and you must flee from him, for he is the father of treachery and despair."

The boy took to heart everything his mother taught him. He told the one called

God how sorrowful he was for the death of the lark, and he made himself a javelin, like those the peasants carried, so that if the devil should come his way, he could do battle with him.

One bright day he heard a thundering noise. The sky was clear but the earth shook as though it were being beaten by storm. It is the devil for sure, he thought and stood, javelin balanced, ready to hurl it at the dreadful foe.

Before long there came into view three mighty warhorses, their hooves hammering the path. Upon their broad backs rode three knights, their armor gleaming like stars fallen from the sky. The boy had never seen such a beautiful sight in his life. This surely was not the devil come into his wilderness. He threw himself facedown upon the ground, blocking the path of the great horses. "If you be God," he cried, "be merciful to me!"

The startled knights jerked their reins

and stopped their horses just short of the boy's body. "Fool!" they cried. "Do you want to be killed?"

But the boy was not offended. "Tell me," he said. "Are you the one called God?"

The knights were amazed. Who was this ignorant boy who mistook three knights for God himself? "Do not bow yourself at our feet. We are not God or gods," the knights said. "We are three men, knights who owe allegiance to Arthur of the Round Table. We are in pursuit of two evil knights who have betrayed the laws of chivalry and taken a young maid captive. In accord with our knightly duty, we are bound to rescue her."

"But what is a knight?" the boy asked. "I know only of one called God and one called the devil. I do not know of knights."

The knights could not believe that in all the world there lived so ignorant a boy.

They told him of the great king and of his knights and their noble quests. Though the boy was a fool, there was something princely in his bearing.

"You are a handsome lad," one of them said at last. "God has clearly marked you with his favor. If I hadn't met you in this wilderness, I would guess that you were a son of kings. Nevertheless, if you wish to be made a knight like us, take yourself to Arthur's court. Now, be good and stand aside, for we must hasten to save this poor maid."

The boy watched the shining men until they disappeared through the trees, and then he ran to tell his mother all that he had seen and heard.

His mother was furious. She sent her son away and called her plowmen and drovers to the cottage. "Why have you failed me?" she asked. "I told you when I came to this place that my son was never to hear the word *knight*, and you swore to me, every last man of you, on pain of death, that you would keep him in ignorance of the court of Arthur and of the life of chivalry."

The peasants hung their heads in sorrow to see their lady so distraught. For they knew that the boy's mother was a queen and his father a king and a knight of Arthur's court. King Gahmuret had died seeking adventure in battle, so Queen Herzoloyde had determined to save her infant son from his father's fate. She had brought him into the wilderness of Soltane, where she thought she could keep him safe.

But the damage was done. The boy was determined to go to Arthur's court and become one of the shining men.

What could the queen do? She wished above all things to keep her son from harm. If I dress him like a fool, she decided, and give him the oldest, most pitiful beast we own, people will laugh at him and he will come running home in shame.

So the queen sewed the boy doublet and breeches made of sackcloth, which came just past his knees. To cover his feet and ankles, she made him buskins of rough, fresh cowhide and found for him a nag so weak with age that Queen Herzoloyde wondered if it could even bear her son's weight as far as the end of the plowed field.

The boy was delighted. What did he know of the world? As always, he trusted his mother to do what was best for him.

"In addition to your clothing and mount, I wish to give you my advice to carry with you," the queen said. And here, she relented a bit, for she did not want him to ride into real danger. She told him to beware crossing swift streams and rivers and to greet everyone he met with courtesy. If a gray-haired man wished to instruct him, he should take heed. She also tried to advise her son about women because clearly he was a handsome boy, just coming into manhood.

"Women will wish to give you a kiss and a token—sometimes a ring or a brooch. Take these; they will cheer you. The love of a good woman is not to be despised. And one more thing I suppose I must tell you, Dear Boy," she said with a sigh. "Beware of the evil knight Lahelin. He and his brother, Orilus, have stolen two kingdoms that should be yours. Lahelin has killed one of your princes and taken many of your people prisoner."

"Never fear, Mother," the boy said, "I will avenge my people with this javelin." She sighed and wept and kissed him good-bye, fearing as she did so that she would never see her beautiful child again.

The boy was proud as a prince, riding through the forest in his fool's clothes on his broken-down nag. But as the day wore on, he got hungry and thirsty and began to look for a place where he might get a meal.

At length, he came upon a lovely pavilion. The boy could not have known that it belonged to one of the very men his mother had warned him of—Duke Orilus. The duke had gone off to hunt with his men, leaving his beautiful wife behind. In the noonday heat, the duchess had taken off her heavy garments, lain down within the tent, and fallen asleep. She did not hear the boy push back the leather curtain and come inside. She awoke with a start to find a youthful stranger in a clownish costume struggling to pull the ring off her hand. She screamed, but the thief showed no alarm.

"Good day, my lady," he said. "My mother told me to give a cheery greeting to everyone I meet. And to take a ring from a good lady if the occasion arose."

The duchess was so frightened she hardly knew how to reply. She begged the stranger to go away and leave her alone.

But he took her ring and helped himself to the brooch he found on her gown. Then he began to complain of hunger. She was afraid of what this muscular youth might do if crossed, so she gave him meat and bread and wine and watched terrified as he devoured the food like a starving beast. Still, she was brave enough to ask that he return her ring and brooch before he went on his way. "They are gifts of my husband," she said, "and he will be furious if you take them."

"Why should he be angry?" the boy said. "I am only doing what my good mother told me to do." And off he went cheerfully on his way, leaving the weeping duchess behind.

The boy followed the road, greeting everyone he passed. "God keep you," he said. "My mother told me to greet you." He was met with many smiles and even laughter, dressed as he was and riding such a wretched mount. But the boy did not know he was being mocked and smiled happily in return.

As he came to a river, he chanced to hear someone crying. He dismounted and went to see whether he could help the person in such distress. There on the farther side of the bank was a young woman, weeping over the body of a knight.

"God keep you, good lady," said the boy. "My mother told me to say that."

The young woman looked up at the strangely clad figure who was greeting her. For all his sackcloth and rawhide leggings, his voice was gentle with compassion.

"Tell me, my lady," he said, wading across the shallow river, dragging his reluctant nag along behind him, "what is the matter? Why do you have such a sad thing in your lap?"

"This is the knight I loved more than life itself," the poor maid said. "And now he is mortally wounded."

"He looks mortally dead to me," said

the boy. "Was it a javelin harmed him? If so, I'll gladly ride out and avenge his death."

The maiden was insulted that the boy should think her noble knight had been brought low by a peasant's dart. Only the coarsest of men would fight with a javelin. "No," she said, "it was a lance. This noble knight lost his life in a joust."

There was something about the rough boy that made the lady look at him more closely. She saw beneath his clothes, fit only for a buffoon, that he was truly well formed and handsome. And there was something quite familiar in his features.

"What is your name?" she asked.

"Oh," he said, "Young Master or Dear Boy or whatever you wish."

"No," she said. "Your true name is Parzival, which means Pierced-through-the-heart, because at your birth your noble mother's heart was truly pierced. I know these things because your mother and mine are sisters. Your father was none other than Gahmuret of Anjou. And through your mother and father, you are heir to three kingdoms. But two brothers, Lahelin and Orilus, have done you wrong. They have stolen your lands and Orilus has slain this knight whom I love."

"I will take my javelin and avenge these wrongs!" Parzival cried. "Just point me the way."

But his cousin feared that the rash boy would get himself killed, so for love of her aunt, she sent him off in the opposite direction.

# Two

# Parzival

S hard as Parzival pressed her, his poor nag could not gallop; indeed, she could hardly toddle forward without stumbling. The day grew old and the shadows long, but the boy rode on. "God keep you!" he called out to everyone—knight or peasant—graybeard or child.

At last the boy felt nearly as spent as his poor beast. He came upon a house where there shone a light at the window and knocked upon the door. A surly face appeared. "God keep you!" the boy said. The man would have slammed the door in his face except that Parzival thrust his javelin in the crack to hold it open. "Kind sir," he said, "my horse and I are very tired and hungrier yet. Would you give us a meal and lodging?"

"Give?" the man snarled. "I give nothing. Show me a coin before you dare ask favors."

"I have no coins," the boy answered. "But a good lady gave me this—" and he held out the gold brooch he had taken from the duchess earlier.

"Ah," said the host, "come in, gentle sir. We will give you food and bed and send you on your way quite satisfied." He reached greedily for the brooch, but Parzival held on to it tightly.

"If you will give me food and fodder for my horse and a place to sleep and then tomorrow lead me to the court of one called Arthur, this brooch shall be yours."

"It would please me to take such a handsome boy to the Round Table," the man said.

The next morning before daybreak,

Parzival roused his host. The boy was so eager to get on his way that he didn't even wait to take breakfast. They rode together until the great city was in sight. Despite his promise, his host refused to go farther. "Won't you take me up and introduce me to the king?" Parzival asked.

"No," the man answered. "I'm only a poor peasant. Those grand knights will despise me."

So, reluctantly, Parzival gave the man the duchess's brooch and rode alone toward the city. In his sackcloth and rawhide and riding bareback astride his broken-down nag, he made quite a sight on the road. Beggar children followed after, shrieking with laughter. "God keep you!" Parzival called to them.

Just then a knight approached. The knight was dressed in red armor. He carried a bright red shield and rode a great sorrel horse—as near to red as a horse can be. In his hand he carried a beautiful goblet of burnished gold.

"God keep you!" Parzival said. "That's what my mother told me to say."

"You are a good lad who does honor to his mother," the knight answered. "I see you are on your way into the city."

"Yes. I am going to Arthur's court to ask him to make me one of his knights."

The Red Knight looked Parzival over, from his sackcloth doublet to his cowhide buskins. He could hardly keep from smiling. "In that case, I would like to ask a favor of you."

"Gladly," the boy said.

"Do you see this goblet? It is from the king's own table. I went to the court to claim my ancestral lands, and"—the knight paused—"carelessly snatched up this goblet. In doing so, I spilled wine on the Lady Guenever's gown. Say this to the king and those in his court—that the Red

Knight is sorry to have insulted the queen by his carelessness. And if any man among them should care to retrieve the king's cup, I stay here waiting for him to come."

Promising to relay the Red Knight's message, Parzival went on toward the city. By the time he entered the city gates, he had drawn quite a crowd. He feared for his little mount, who was being shoved this way and that. She stumbled to her bony knees more than once, and each time she fell, Parzival was forced to dismount and pull her to her feet as the mob roared with laughter.

When the raucous procession had forced its way into the courtyard of the castle, knights and nobles came tumbling out the doorways to see the cause of the disturbance.

Parzival called out to them all, "God keep you! That is what my mother told me to say." He had to yell to be heard above the jeering of the crowd. "But which of you is Arthur? I see many Arthurs here! Where is the one who will make me a knight?"

Iwanet, a page about Parzival's age, took pity on the boy. He ran forward and took the reins of the nag and bade Parzival to dismount. "The king is not out here in the courtyard," he said. "I will take you in to see him as soon as I have stabled your horse."

"My mother bade me give a special greeting to Arthur and his lady!" yelled Parzival, still trying to make himself heard over the noise of the crowd. "And I have another message as well. A knight that I met outside the city says he is waiting for someone to come and fetch the king's cup. Can that mean he wants to fight? Oh, yes, and he's sorry, too, that he spilled wine upon the queen. He was dressed in red. I wish I had such armor."

Iwanet grabbed Parzival by the arm and dragged him away from the hoots of the crowd and into the castle. There the mocking ceased, for those within looked past his fool's rags. The boy they saw was of such beauty and noble bearing that most suspected at once that he was the son of a king in disguise.

"God keep you, sir, and your lady, too," Parzival said when he came into the king's presence. "My mother told me to give you a special greeting."

"What do you want from me, my lad?" Arthur asked, his voice as kindly as his bearing.

"Make me a knight!" the boy said at once. "It feels like years since I determined to become one. I can't wait any longer. And I don't ask anything of you but your leave. A knight I met upon the road into the city has wonderful red armor, which I should love to have. If I can't take his, then I shan't take anything from the king."

"My lad," the king said, "that knight you speak of would not easily give up his armor. He is very powerful. Indeed, he is making my life miserable because he thinks I have not given him his due. I can't send an untried boy against Sir Ither, the Red Knight."

But Arthur had a wily counselor named Sir Kay, who whispered in the king's ear. "Send out the boy, my lord. He and Ither will just knock about a bit. The boy has to learn about these things if he is to be a knight." In truth, Sir Kay cared about neither Sir Ither's nor Parzival's life.

"I do not want the boy to be killed," said the king. But seeing how determined the boy was, he finally gave him leave to go.

Parzival was racing out of the castle when a strange thing happened. There was a princess in the court, the sister of those same brothers, Orilus and Lahelin, who had stolen the kingdoms of Parzival's father. This princess had sworn not to laugh until she met the noblest knight in the land—the winner of many jousts. When she saw

Parzival running out of the court in his sackcloth clothes and cowhide leggings, she laughed out loud without thinking.

Sir Kay was enraged. The princess had refused to laugh at all the noble knights who had sought her favor, and now she had laughed at this foolish boy. "You have shamed the court!" Sir Kay shouted, grabbing her by the hair. "You have made a fool of yourself and all of us by your unseemly behavior." When a young knight sprang to the lady's defense, Sir Kay beat them both.

Poor Parzival was dismayed. He had no idea that the princess was the sister of his sworn enemies, but that would not have mattered. The boy's heart was tender toward any defenseless creature who had suffered because of him. He wanted to hurl his javelin at Sir Kay, but there was too great a crowd for him to do so.

I shall not come back to this court, he

vowed to himself, until I make amends for the wrong done to this poor lady.

The Red Knight was surprised to see Parzival coming toward him, riding his pitiful little horse. He had been expecting a joust with one of the knights of the Round Table. "God keep you, sir," Parzival called out. "The king has given me your mount and your armor. And if you are wise, you'll hand them over at once."

"If the king gave you my armor," the Red Knight answered, "he has given *me* your life. I wonder what you've done in the past to deserve such a favor from the king."

"Stop your chatter and give me your armor," Parzival said, and he grabbed the reins of Ither's horse. "You are Lahelin, aren't you? The enemy about whom my mother warned me."

The angry Ither jerked his reins from the boy's hands and gave Parzival such a blow with his lance that his poor little horse fell to the ground. Then the Red Knight beat the boy with the shaft of his lance until the blood gushed. At first, Parzival could not move under the blows, but as soon as he could, he raised his javelin and hurled it through the gap in Sir Ither's helmet.

The Red Knight fell to the ground. Seeing that his enemy was quite dead, Parzival began tugging at the Red Knight's armor. But pull and struggle and twist as he might, he couldn't wrestle the armor off the knight's body.

At about that time, Iwanet, the page, came running up, having followed Parzival from the city. Iwanet was amazed to see the great knight dead and Parzival yanking and tugging at Sir Ither's armor.

"God keep you!" Parzival said. "Now how do I get this armor off this knight and onto me?"

Iwanet helped Parzival unfasten the armor and remove it from the dead knight's body. "Take off your buskins," he said to Parzival. "They have no place under a knight's armor."

But Parzival refused. "No," he said. "My mother made them. I won't discard anything that my mother made for me so lovingly." Iwanet sighed, but there was no way to change Parzival's mind, so he helped him don the Red Knight's gleaming armor on top of his sackcloth and raw leather.

But when Parzival asked the page to hand him his quiver of javelins, Iwanet refused. "The order of chivalry forbids javelins," the page said. "Take instead the sword and lance of the Red Knight. These are the weapons of chivalry."

Parzival did as Iwanet commanded, buckling on the great sword of Ither and fastening the lance to the shield as Iwanet directed. Then, impatient to be off, Parzival leapt unaided into the saddle of the

Red Knight's horse. "Take the goblet to the king and give him my greeting," he said to Iwanet. "I myself can't enter the court, for I have caused a lady to be humiliated on my account. I'm too ashamed to return."

Iwanet made a cross out of the javelin that had killed poor Ither to mark the site of his death and then threw the rest of the quiver away. The knight's body was later carried back to the castle, where all the ladies wept that one so handsome and brave should die without honor—slain by a mere dart in the hand of a raw and foolish boy.

Meantime, the great sorrel horse had carried Parzival far away until it came to the castle of a prince named Gurnemanz. The prince had lost three sons in battle, so when he saw Parzival at his door, his heart went out to the youth as though Providence had sent a fourth son into his life.

"God keep you!" Parzival said upon meeting the prince. "My mother told me to seek advice from a man whose hair is gray. If you will teach me to be wise, I will serve you as my mother told me to."

Prince Gurnemanz was overjoyed. "Tell me about yourself," the prince asked. "Where have you come from?"

Then Parzival told the prince about his mother and how he had left her; about how he got a ring and a brooch; how he had caused a princess much pain; and how he had won his armor. These stories made the prince sigh. "Was I wrong?" the boy asked. "Shouldn't I do as my mother instructed me? Why should Sir Kay treat the princess so harshly? And why did Iwanet refuse me my javelins?"

Gurnemanz's noble heart sank as he listened to Parzival prattle on. For the sake of the code of chivalry and the boy's own safety, he must begin at once to teach Parzival how to be a proper knight.

The prince's first task was to persuade Parzival not to wear under his armor the sackcloth clothes and cowhide buskins his mother had made him, but to put on garments of silk and wool, worthy of the son of a king. Next, the prince took him to the jousting field and taught him how to use his sword and lance. Parzival was quick to learn and soon unhorsed all the opponents the prince sent against him.

Prince Gurnemanz also taught him proper manners. He urged him to be humble and discreet among nobility and to be compassionate toward the poor and needy—to hold ladies in high esteem and to temper daring with mercy. "If you have defeated a man in battle," the prince said, "you do not need to kill him. Never kill, my son, unless you must."

Parzival remembered the lark and the Red Knight and felt fresh sorrow for their deaths.

"And, my son, you must not constantly

speak of your mother. It makes you seem like a child. Nor"—and here he sighed—"nor must you ask so many questions. When you ask questions, you make people think you are a simpleton."

He begged Parzival to stay on at his castle, to marry his daughter and become in reality his son. But Parzival was impatient for adventure. "I'm not ready to marry, for I still have much to do before I come to man's estate," he told the prince. "When I am a famous knight, I shall come back and ask you for the hand of your pretty Liaze." Parzival did not mean to lie, but he knew nothing of what lay ahead or that his heart would soon tread quite a different path.

Few horses known could travel as fast as the great sorrel, so it was by evening that Parzival found himself on the bank of a roaring river. On the other side of the river gorge was a walled city, and the only way to the city was by a bridge made of rope strung across the raging torrent. Before the gates of the city, Parzival saw more than fifty knights armed and helmeted for battle. When the knights realized that Parzival meant to cross over to the city, they cried out, "Go back! Go back!"

But Parzival urged his steed forward. Their first few steps out on the woven bridge made the whole span swing wildly from side to side. As fearless as he was in battle, at the sight of this bridge, the brave sorrel shied and would not go on. At length, Parzival dismounted and slowly eased himself and his terrified mount across the treacherous suspension. By the time they got to the other side of the chasm, the knights had disappeared and there was no light to be seen.

The gates of the darkened city were bolted, and at first no one answered his call or his knocking. But, at last, a tiny window in the wall opened and a young girl looked out. She thrust a lantern out of the opening to see who had knocked and saw the handsome Parzival below. "If you come as an enemy," she called down to him, "I pray you be gone, for we have suffered enough from our enemies. If you come for shelter and food, we cannot help you, for the city has been under siege for many weeks and there is no food within these gates. It will be best if you go and leave us to die."

Now Parzival remembered Gurnemanz's teaching that a knight's duty was to help those in need, so he said, "I have come for nothing but to offer my help to the king and people of this city."

"Our king has died," the girl said. "And it is for love of his daughter, our new queen, that we suffer. She will not give herself in marriage to her enemy, King Clamide, and he is determined to destroy us unless she relents."

Parzival persuaded the girl to let him in and take him to the queen so that he could offer himself in her service. As he walked through the narrow streets, Parzival's heart was moved to pity. Even in the dim light of the maiden's lantern, he could see that the people were as pale and weak as plants that have never seen the sunlight. Children stared at his shining red armor with great sad eyes, but no one had the strength to greet him.

The girl led Parzival as far as the castle, where the queen's guard took him into a garden. There, he removed his armor and washed the rust off his body. Clean garments were brought for him to put on, for even in this sad city, courtesy was not forgotten.

At length, Parzival was led into the throne room. The nobles and their ladies were nearly as wretched and weak as the peasants he had seen in the streets. But pale and thin as she was, there stood one whose beauty shone dazzling as the evening star. Even as Parzival stared at her,

Condwiramurs the queen came toward him, kissed him on the cheek, and took his hand to lead him to where he was to sit down beside her.

Parzival sat without speaking. He remembered that Gurnemanz had warned him not to ask questions, and he was determined that he would behave in a manner befitting a knight in the presence of this lovely queen.

At last the queen spoke. "I am told that you have offered me your service. It has been a long time since a stranger has come to offer us help. Who are you, sir, and where have you come from?"

"I am Parzival the son of Gahmuret, my lady. And today I have come from the castle of a kind prince named Gurnemanz, to whom I owe much."

"I am amazed and overjoyed to hear you say this," she said. "Amazed because the trip to my uncle's home is a two-day journey and you have accomplished it in one. And overjoyed to hear that you have come from my mother's brother. His daughter, Liaze, and I have shared many a sad tear. Indeed, her brother died seeking to defend me from this villain who has stolen all my lands and now besieges this city, which is all that remains of my father's kingdom. As I have just told my kinsmen"—she indicated two monks who stood nearby—"we are at the point of famine here. I cannot even offer you the entertainment that a guest of your stature is due."

When she said this, the two monks offered to return to their homes in the country and send food so that a proper feast might be prepared for her noble guest. The queen accepted this offer gladly, but when the food for the feast arrived, Parzival insisted that it be divided so that all the people might have something to eat.

The people loved Parzival for this, the

queen most of all, for it broke her heart to see her people suffer. "I would rather die," she told him, "than marry Clamide, who has slaughtered my warriors and starved my people."

"How then can I serve you?"

"We have had word that Clamide's chief officer, Kingrum, will arrive tomorrow at the head of a large army. They are coming from the west, where the river cannot protect us. I fear all is lost," she said.

But on the next morning Parzival donned his shining red armor and spurred the red sorrel out of the castle toward the advancing foe. Kingrum, seeing a lone knight coming, spurred his horse, too, so that the two of them met. This was Parzival's first sword fight, but Gurnemanz had taught him well. He returned Kingrum blow for blow until at last he had hurled the older man upon the ground and stood over him ready for the death blow.

Kingrum pled for mercy, and Parzival,

remembering the teaching of Gurnemanz, relented. "I shall give you your life," he said, "if you will present yourself to Prince Gurnemanz."

Kingrum was alarmed. "Then you might as well kill me now," he said, "for I killed his son. What will he do to me?"

"I will give you another choice, then," said Parzival. "Go to Arthur's court. There is a lady there who suffered humiliation because of me. Kneel to her, the Lady Cunneware, and say to her and to the king and all the court that I will not return until I have cleansed the dishonor that we share."

Kingrum was happy to escape with his life and hurried to the court of Arthur to fulfill this pledge.

That night a wonderful thing happened. Two ships foundered on the rocks of the river—ships whose sole cargo was food. In their desperation, Queen Condwiramurs's hungry people would have plundered the ships, but Parzival held them back and gathered gold and jewels from the castle to pay the merchant seamen for their cargo. Then he carefully parceled out all the food, so that no one would have too little or too much.

Another wonderful thing happened that very night. Queen Condwiramurs, who had loved Parzival for his beauty, now loved him for his wisdom and generosity. Before the sun set, she took the son of Gahmuret to be her husband and her king.

A few days later, King Clamide, who had heard nothing of these things, set out for Queen Condwiramurs's city, determined to subdue it once and for all and to force the queen to be his bride.

He moved slowly, for his army was a large one. Long before he had reached the city, he was met by a page from the forces that had set out under Kingrum, his steward. The page told Clamide how a great Red Knight had defeated Kingrum and sent the steward to Arthur's court. Clamide was furious because he thought Cond-wiramurs had sent for Sir Ither to be her champion. That cursed knight, he thought, always did have a way with women.

Clamide was more determined than ever to lay waste the city and take the queen for his own. Kingrum sent me word, he said to himself, that the people are starving. How can they hold out against me any longer?

Before long, a knight from Kingrum's forces came riding up in great distress, telling him the same story that the page had. But Clamide would not give up. He urged his men forward. He did not know, of course, that the city now had food aplenty and new heart since Parzival had become the king.

The battle was fierce and Clamide's forces were taken by surprise. This was not the starving army of hopeless men they had expected.

That first day, many of Clamide's men were taken prisoner. "Bring them within the city gates and take good care of them," Parzival ordered. For three days, the prisoners received good food and tender care for their wounds. Then, stripped of their weapons, they were let go.

When they returned to their units, their fellow soldiers greeted them with pity. "You must be starving," they said, "locked up in that famine-ridden city."

"Don't feel sorry for us," the prisoners said. "We were treated royally in there. They've got enough food in that city to last out a year of siege."

When Clamide heard this report, he realized that further siege would be useless, so he sent word to the city that if there was one inside who would dare meet him, Clamide, in single combat, the two of them could settle matters once and for all.

Of course, this was just what Parzival

had hoped for. He and Clamide met in the center of the field. They fought until both horses foundered from fatigue, and then they jumped down and continued the battle on foot. Parzival struck his foe with such a rain of blows that Clamide cried out: "This is to be single combat! You must call off your rocks and your catapult!"

Parzival laughed. "We have sent no rocks or catapult against you. I gave my word on that. There is only *this* machine of war." He raised his sword arm again. "Would you like to ask me to protect you from that?"

Clamide was so tired that he could fight no longer. He took one final blow to the helmet and fell to the ground, waiting for the stroke that would mean his death.

Parzival raised his arm once more. This was the man who had cost his wife so much pain. "You will never live to grieve my wife again," he said.

"Why should you kill me?" the unlucky

Clamide said. "You have won everything—a kingdom, the woman I love, and all my honor."

Slowly, Parzival lowered his sword. *Do not kill unless you must,* Gurnemanz had said. "I will let you go," he said, "if you will submit yourself to Prince Gurnemanz."

"Then kill me now," Clamide replied, "for I have done that prince a wrong he will not forgive. I have besieged the kingdom of his niece. His own son died in defense of this city. Do not send me to Gurnemanz. If I must die, kill me now with your own sword."

"Go, then, to Arthur's court," Parzival said. "Greet the king for me and give your service to a lady who has suffered much because of me." And so Clamide, too, was sent to serve Cunneware. And you may guess that Sir Kay was not happy to see two such warriors sent from Parzival to the service of the woman he had wronged.

Queen Condwiramurs's city rejoiced as

only those who have known great grief can rejoice, and Parzival and Condwiramurs lived together in great happiness. They were wise and generous rulers, so the life of that place was truly good for all the people.

Then the day came when Parzival said to his queen, "I must go and see how my mother is. For I have had no word from her these many months—and if by chance I meet adventure along the way, well, that is the calling of a knight, isn't it?"

Because she loved him so much, she let him go, but she could not keep from weeping as she watched him ride away, his only companion the great red sorrel.

# Three
❧
# Wild Mountain

HAT day, Parzival's thoughts as he rode were not on his journey but on the queen whom he had left behind. Thus, he forgot to guide the great sorrel's way and was led, as though by the hand of God, into a dense forest, which was known in those parts as the Land of Wildness.

Near evening, he came upon a lake, and there upon the lake were boats. Parzival rode up to the boat closest to the shore. In it, propped up against the stern, was a handsomely dressed man, his hat lined with peacock feathers, who was casting his line into the water.

This is no ordinary fisherman, thought Parzival to himself. But, remembering Gurnemanz's teaching, he restrained his curiosity, and greeting the man with quiet courtesy, he asked if there was a place nearby where he might spend the night.

The fisherman looked up into the young man's face and then said slowly, as though he were in great pain or sorrow, "There is no place a day's ride from here except that great castle you have just passed."

Parzival was surprised. He remembered no castle, but when he turned, there behind him on a high hill were the towers and turrets of what had to be a mighty fortress.

"The name of the place you see up there is Wild Mountain, and when you call at the drawbridge," the man said, "tell them that the Angler has sent you, and they will take you in."

Parzival did as he was told, and when he called out that the Angler had sent him, the drawbridge was immediately let down and the huge iron gates swung open. Solemn pages crowded around him to tend his horse. Others led him to a spacious chamber and helped him out of his armor. They bathed the rust from his body with warm water and anointed it with sweet-smelling oils. The lady of the castle had sent a robe of Arabic gold for him to wear. It was no less than the master of the wardrobe himself who helped Parzival put on the robe. Wine was brought and grapes and pomegranates the color of jewels. Still, in all this splendid welcome, there was neither a smile nor a laugh. A strange sorrow hung like a veil of mourning over all whom he met.

Solemn-faced knights came to invite him into the great hall. "The Angler is here," they said. The hall was as large as the hall of Arthur's court and, if anything, more splendid. Everyone—lord, lady, or servant—was dressed as though for a glorious feast day, but there was no joy of festival in the castle of Wild Mountain.

At the far end of the great hall, propped against rich cushions of silk and velvet and robes of sable and ermine, near to the great fireplace, reclined the Angler King of Wild Mountain. Perhaps this was the reason for the sadness all around him, for the king seemed to be in great pain. In a weak voice, the king bade him come into the hall. "Come sit down by me," he said.

Parzival did as the king asked, marveling at the strangeness of the scene. Though the fire blazed hot, the king lay shivering in his furs. Suddenly, the door at the far end of the hall was thrown open. A page ran in, carrying in his hand a lance. The page ran to each of the four corners of the hall and as he did so, Parzival could hear the knights and ladies and servants begin to weep. As the page ran past the place where Parzival sat, he saw that blood was dripping from the point of the lance. Then the page ran out and the door was shut behind him.

Before Parzival could wonder more about this peculiar ceremony, the doors were once again thrown open. Through them came four beautiful maidens carrying golden candlesticks. Two noblewomen followed, carrying ivory stands. Next, eight young maidens, four bearing more candles and four bearing a great jewel—a garnet that had been cut to form a tabletop. The garnet was put on the ivory stands to make a table for the king to dine upon. Six maidens brought in silver knives, which they laid out on the garnet tabletop.

And then, most wonderful of all, came four more maidens with crystal lamps, followed by a princess who carried in her hands that sacred vessel that few have ever seen, and of which Parzival had never heard. As the Grail approached, Parzival heard the king groan as though he were in mortal pain.

The princess placed the Grail on the king's table and then she and her ladies stepped back. Servants came and brought tables for all the guests. Gold dishes and goblets were brought for all as well.

A page carried to the king's table a golden basin and silken towel. The king washed his hands and bade Parzival to wash. All was prepared for a great feast, but where was the food and drink?

Just then, the servant behind Parzival held out a goblet toward the Grail. Immediately it was filled, and the servant set before Parzival a golden vessel filled with rich, red wine. Then he held out the golden dish and set it down before Parzival. It was overflowing with meats and fruits and rich foods of every kind. One by one the servants did this, and so served the king and his guests a banquet so sumptuous that even those in Arthur's court would have been amazed.

What can this be? What is the meaning of these strange events? Parzival wondered, but he remembered kind Gurnemanz's advice not to ask questions. Surely, if I am patient, everything will be revealed to me, he thought.

As he was thinking this, a page came toward the king bearing a sword. The sword was sheathed in gold and its hilt was a single ruby. The king motioned that the page was to present the sword to Parzival. "Before God crippled me, I carried this sword in many a great battle. Since I have only been able to offer you the poorest of hospitality, take this sword. I think you will find that it will serve you well."

As he took the sword into his hands, Parzival felt all the eyes in the hall on him.

And all of them sorrowful, especially those of the king, but he remembered Gurnemanz's warning and did not ask why.

The feasting was at an end. The servants removed the dishes and goblets and then the tables. The maidens and noble ladies took out the lamps, the candlesticks, the silver knives, the garnet tabletop, the ivory stands, and last of all the Grail.

The king wished Parzival good night, like the courteous host that he was. Knights led Parzival to his bedchamber. Pages undressed him and put him in a canopied bed, where maidens brought him grapes and mulberry wine and bade him rest well.

Though Parzival was very tired, he tossed and turned, churning to troubled dreams of swords cutting his flesh and lances piercing his body.

When he awoke with a start, the sun was shining through his window. He waited for the pages or the knights or the master of the wardrobe to come in and dress him for the day. But the castle was deathly still. He sat up in bed. His underclothing and armor were laid out for him. He realized at once that he was meant to dress himself. He jumped up in alarm. Something dreadful must have happened.

He threw on his underclothing and armed himself as quickly as he could with no one to help. I must find the king and offer him my service, he thought. But he wandered from room to room and could find no one.

He yelled out as loudly as he could, but the sound of his own voice echoed in the empty air.

Finally, he went out the great castle door, and there at the bottom of the steps stood his horse, saddled and bridled. Someone had propped his sword and lance against the sorrel's flank. By now Parzival was more angry than concerned.

He ran out to the courtyard where he had been greeted so courteously the night before. It was as empty as the castle, but he could see that the grass had been trampled, as though many horsemen had mounted there not long before. He raced back to the sorrel and leapt into the saddle. The gate was open and the drawbridge down.

He galloped across, but when he got to the end of the drawbridge, someone behind him yanked the cable so abruptly that Parzival was nearly thrown, horse and all, into the moat. Parzival turned back to see who had done this to him.

There, standing in the open gateway, was the page who had pulled the cable, shaking his fist at Parzival. "May God damn the light that falls on your path!" the boy cried. "You fool! You wretched fool! Why didn't you ask the question?"

"What do you mean?" Parzival shouted back. "What question?"

Without another word, the page turned on his heel and disappeared. At once the iron portcullis crashed down upon the stone pavement. Parzival was alone.

There was nothing for him to do but to go forward, following the tracks of those who had left the yard earlier. Perhaps the king's men are engaged in a battle, he thought. I can join them and offer the service of this great sword that the king has given me. Maybe they think I am a coward and that is why they despise me.

He followed the tracks, riding hard, but the hoofprints began to split off until at last they disappeared altogether. It was then that he heard the sound of a woman weeping. He followed the sound and found a young woman sitting against a linden tree, cradling in her arms the body of a knight, which had been embalmed.

At first Parzival did not recognize her, for she had shaved her head and was dressed in the rough clothes of a peasant.

"May I be of service to you, madam?" he asked.

"No, no one can help me," the young woman said. "For I am grieving more each day. But where did you come from? This is the Land of Wildness and not safe for travelers."

"I came today from the castle called Wild Mountain," Parzival said. "I passed the night there in some splendor."

The young woman looked startled. "You must be jesting," she said. "No one comes upon Wild Mountain by chance. Only those who are meant to find it are brought to it. You are a stranger here. Perhaps you do not know then about King Anfortas the son of Frimutel."

Parzival confessed that he did not know this king, so the young woman continued. "Anfortus is the eldest of five noble children. One is long dead, and three of them live on in misery. The fifth, Trevrizent, is a hermit, who has chosen the path of poverty for God's sake. Anfortas, for all his wealth, lives in great pain. He can neither sit up nor lie down, neither ride nor walk. Even propped among his pillows, the agony is more than he can bear. If only you had been the one. If only you had seen him, you could have rid him of his suffering."

"But I did see him," Parzival said. "I saw the king and many wonderful and strange things there in Wild Mountain."

"Why," she said, "you are Parzival. I did not recognize you in the armor of a knight. Do you remember me? I am your cousin Sigune, whom you met on the road to Arthur's court. I told you your true name. And since that day, you have been to Wild Mountain. Then tell me the good news. Tell me that the king is healed."

"Can you be my cousin Sigune? I didn't recognize you; you've grown so pale, and

what has become of your beautiful hair?
Come, Cousin, let me help you bury this
knight."

"There is only one thing on earth that
could ease my pain," Sigune said. "Tell me
that the king is released from his. I see his
sword bound at your waist. Dear Cousin,
the marvels you have seen are nothing
compared to those that are to come to
you if"—she looked up into Parzival's face—
"if you asked the question."

"What question, Cousin?"

Sigune's pale face grew whiter still. "I
cannot believe it. You were taken to Wild
Mountain. You saw the marvels of that
place. You saw the Grail itself and the
awful suffering of its king—and you did
not ask the question?"

Parzival was alarmed by the change
in his cousin's manner. "What question
should I have asked? Tell me. I don't
understand."

"Get away from my sight. I can't abide

to have you in my vision, you perfidious knight," she said. "Have you no shred of compassion?" The woman was wild with rage. "You may live, but in the reckoning of Heaven, you are already dead!"

"Dear Cousin," Parzival pleaded. "Please. I promise you, whatever I may have done, I'll make amends."

"Do you think to make the amends of a knight?" she asked, her voice cruel with sarcasm. "There are no amends for what you have failed to do. There is no longer need for you to follow the rules of chivalry. You were shorn of all knightly honor at Wild Mountain." Sigune turned away from Parzival, her eyes on the pitiful figure in her lap. When she spoke again, her voice was so low that Parzival had to bend down to hear her words. "I will not, I cannot say another word to you," she said. "Go. My only hope in this world is that I will never again have to look upon your face."

# Four

## Under Curse

**HEN** Parzival saw that it was useless to plead with his cousin, he mounted the sorrel and spurred him to a gallop, wanting only to leave this cursed place of sickness and death. But the farther he rode, the more the grief he had left behind crowded the narrow spaces of his heart.

No amends! How could that be? He had meant no wrong. Indeed, all he desired was to be a man of knightly honor and courtesy—to be a man of whom his wife, his mother, and his foster father, Gurnemanz, could be proud—and it had brought only disaster. Bathed in perspiration, Parzival took off his helmet and slowed his sorrel to a trot.

Suddenly, he saw ahead of him in the road a sorry sight. It might once have been a horse, but now the poor creature was nothing but bones with skin stretched over them, and the skin itself was near worn through. He recalled the nag his mother had given him those days long ago when he was a raw and happy boy. Why, that old mare would look like a mighty warhorse compared to this wretched beast.

Parzival had had no warning that there were another horse and rider ahead. Now he saw why. Every bell had been ripped from the sad beast's saddle. Indeed, the saddle itself no longer fit the horse's poor, swayed back; and more pitiful than the mount was the rider. It was a woman, but she wore no gown, only a tattered shift, belted with a piece of rope.

When Parzival came alongside her, she

looked at him with alarm and covered herself with her arms. "Go away and leave me alone," she said. "I saw you once before, and since that terrible day I have had nothing but misery on your account."

"My lady," Parzival said, "whatever I have done or left undone, since I have become a knight no one could say that I have ever been unkind to a lady."

"You were most unkind to me," she said. "You would have my ring and my brooch. And see what has become of me because of that."

"Madam," Parzival said, recognizing the duchess he had met on that day he left home in search of Arthur's court, "let me cover you with my cloak and then I will make amends for this wrong I did when I was but a foolish boy."

"Leave me," she cried. "Or my husband will return and kill us both."

In fact, the jealous Duke Orilus had

already heard the sorrel's whinny and was returning to see who had met his wife along the path. Quickly, Parzival put on his helmet and spurred forward to meet the duke. The poor duchess was distraught. As much as Parzival had wronged her and her husband had punished her unjustly, she did not wish either man to die on her account.

It looked as though someone was sure to die, the fighting was so fierce. Part of the duke's fury was his own guilt that he had left his wife unprotected that time before when, as he thought, she had given a stranger her favors. Now he fought like the very dragons that adorned his shield. Parzival was his equal in fury, determined to make amends, at least for the childish behavior that had caused the duchess so much humiliation and pain.

They struck at each other with lance and sword, charging until both horses were in a lather. But neither man could unhorse the other. The duke, in desperation, snatched hold of a buckle on Parzival's armor, but the strong young knight grabbed the duke around the waist, hoisted him from the saddle, and hurled him through the air as though he were a bundle of twigs.

Parzival leapt off the sorrel and raced to where the duke lay gasping upon the ground.

"You have humiliated this good lady without a cause," Parzival cried. "If you will not restore her to favor and give her back her good name, I will not let you live!"

"I cannot do that," Duke Orilus replied. "She has given me too much grief—betraying me with some stranger in the woods."

"Then you are lost." Parzival raised his sword.

The duke did not want to die and said so.

Parzival lowered his sword arm. "There is a lady in Arthur's court who has suffered humiliation on my account," he said. "Go there and say that the Red Knight has sent you to offer her your service."

"That I will do and gladly," the duke answered.

"But," said Parzival, "that is not all. I cannot let you go unless you repent of your wrong to this good lady, your wife."

When the duke saw that Parzival would not relent, he swore finally that he would restore his wife to favor. Parzival let him stand and returned to him his sword and lance.

"Now that you have sworn," Parzival said, "I will tell you that this lady is completely innocent of any wrongdoing. I know, for I was that foolish youth. Here is the ring I took from her against her will. The brooch, I'm sorry to say, is gone. I gave it in payment to a greedy man. You, sir, have nothing to forgive. Your wife has never betrayed you. I only pray that she will forgive us both."

This the good duchess was glad to do. Her husband wept to think of the wrong his jealousy had caused. He gave her back her lovely garments and procured a beautiful mare for her to ride, its saddle trimmed with hundreds of silver bells. Duke Orilus and his duchess asked Parzival to go with them to Arthur's court, but he sadly refused. His cousin had told him that his failure at Wild Mountain stripped him of all knightly honor. How could such a one approach the noble Arthur? He bade the now happy duke and duchess farewell.

Parzival traveled alone for many a weary day. It began to snow, though it was not long past the feast of St. Michael and the Angels and so not yet winter. To Parzival, night and day, summer and winter were the same dreary time. He mounted his horse at dawn and rode past dark, but he did not know where he was going.

Nor did he know that Arthur had ridden out from the court at Camelot with his queen and a large company of knights and ladies. The king had decreed that this would be a time of hunting and pleasure. No one was to joust or seek adventure in battle. Arthur's men had made a camp of bright-colored pavilions with banners flying. The word of this encampment soon spread through the countryside, so that Duke Orilus and his duchess quite easily found their way there. When the duke sought the lady to whom he was to offer his service, he found to his surprise that it was his own sister. As for Sir Kay, that knight was somewhat disquieted to realize that the foolish youth he had despised had sent yet a third knight to Lady Cunneware's protection.

Since Parzival did not know that the king of the Britons was encamped nearby, he had no way of knowing when he woke up that snowy morning that one of the king's falcons had flown out from its falconer the day before and had not returned. This same bird was in the tree above his head, and when he set out on his day of aimless travel, the bird, who felt at home in the company of knights, followed him.

The two of them, lost knight and lost bird, traveled together. The knight's way was the harder, for the snow had covered any semblance of a path, and his horse would often stumble on rocks and fallen branches. At length they came to a clearing in the forest. There in the clearing was a flock of wild geese who, pausing on their southward journey, were searching the frozen ground for food. The falcon hurled itself like a stone from the sky upon the throat of one of the geese. The goose wrung itself free and, in a thrashing of wild wings, all the geese flew up and escaped. But the wounded goose left behind three drops of blood, bright red upon the snow.

Parzival stared at the blood as though dazed. Somehow, in those three drops he saw the warm cheeks and bright mouth of Condwiramurs, his wife. With all that had happened since he had ridden away from her, her face had grown dim, but now, staring at the snow, her lovely face was all that he could see. He could not take his eyes away, nor did he want to. He was like a senseless man, imprisoned in a dream.

Now it chanced that Arthur's court was encamped hardly more than a javelin's throw from that very spot. Just then a servant boy, who belonged to that same Lady Cunneware whom Parzival had vowed to help, came through the clearing on the way to run an errand for his mistress. He did not recognize his lady's champion, now a knight in fine red armor. He ran as fast as he could through the snow back to the encampment to raise an alarm.

"Help!" he cried. "Help! There is a strange knight just on the other side of the camp. His helmet is badly dented and his shield is hacked by many conflicts. He's come to threaten the king!" the boy shouted. "Shame on you, all you cowardly knights!"

Now every knight in the encampment wanted to rush out at once and dispatch this evil knight, but since Arthur had forbidden battle, they could not go until the king had released them from the ban against jousting.

The king and queen, however, were still sound asleep in their pavilion, so what should the eager knights do? Young Segramors, who was the queen's kinsman, simply pushed aside the curtain and went straight into the king's tent. He woke up the king and queen, and, hardly apologizing for his rudeness, told them what the servant boy had said and asked permission to challenge the mysterious stranger.

Arthur was angry both at the intrusion and the request. "If I let you go after I have expressly forbidden warfare at this place, everyone will want to joust and do battle. There'll be no end to it."

But Guenever was fond of her young cousin. She wanted him to gain honor in the sight of the Round Table knights, so she coaxed and pleaded until, finally, the king gave the young knight leave to go.

Segramors was delighted. He had himself armed as quickly as possible and followed Cunneware's servant boy to the place just beyond the camp. There they spied poor Parzival still staring at the drops of blood upon the snow.

Segramors called out to him. "I do not know who you are, sir, but you should know that you have no business here. Why, it is almost as though you cannot see just yonder in plain sight the tents of a king encamped there with his many knights. You are foolish to threaten him thus. Surrender yourself to me now and save your life."

Parzival, lost in the sickness of love, did not even hear this challenge. Segramors called out again, but still the visitor was silent. Indeed, he did not even turn his head to acknowledge Segramors's threat.

Segramors spurred his horse into a gallop. At this, the sorrel whirled to spare his own life. As the horse turned him about, Parzival lost sight of the blood drops and found himself being borne down upon by a charging knight. He weighed his lance and knocked the startled Segramors right over the rump of his horse and into the snow.

The other knights, gathered at the edge of the clearing, could see Segramors dumped backward over his horse's crupper. They waited, hardly breathing, for the strange knight to leap off his own horse and end the battle, but the visitor had already turned his back on Sir Segramors. What arrogance! The knights sent pages to pull the prone Segramors to his feet and lead him to his tent, where he could repair his wounded dignity. The knights themselves rushed to Arthur's pavilion, all clamoring at once for leave to dispatch this haughty interloper.

It was Sir Kay who prevailed. His reputation for gallantry had been in doubt ever since that unfortunate day when he had beaten Lady Cunneware. "My Lord," he said, "if you do not give me leave to trounce this menace once and for all, I will resign from your service. There he waits— waving his lance in sight of the queen. He is disgracing us all." So Arthur gave his steward permission to challenge the stranger, perhaps thinking that Sir Kay had much to redeem since there were now three knights at court with the sworn duty to see that Sir Kay minded his manners.

Sir Kay took time to have his horse groomed and his armor polished. Then he sallied forth to the clearing with his pages in attendance and his banners streaming.

"Sir," he called out to Parzival, "you must know that you have insulted the king of Britain and his lady. You will not get by so easily with me as you did with that green boy who challenged you earlier. Turn and surrender at once, else it will go very hard for you."

Parzival did not turn, nor did he answer a word to this bold challenge. This made Kay furious. He rode forward and whacked Parzival's helmet with his lance so hard that it rang like a bell. The sorrel spun around at the sound. "Now," cried Sir Kay, "I will beat you like a miller beats his donkey!" He trotted his horse to the edge of the clearing, then spurred it into a full gallop.

When the sorrel turned, Parzival's trance once again was broken. He awoke just in time to see a second knight charging toward him at full tilt. Sir Kay thrust his lance straight through Parzival's shield, but Parzival struck back, knocking Sir Kay right off his mount. The unlucky steward fell against a tree, breaking both an arm and a leg.

As for Parzival, he turned once more to stare at the ruby drops upon the snow. He did not even notice the hole in his shield or that he had shattered his lance in the joust.

Sir Kay was carried on a pallet to Arthur's pavilion, where all the court crowded about him, lamenting his injuries, kindly Sir Gawain most of all.

"Well, of course," Sir Kay said sarcastically to Gawain, "it would not do for you to ride out to avenge me. I am only the king's steward and you are the king's own nephew. It would not be proper for you to lower yourself to combat on my account. If the situation were reversed, if even the toe on your foot had been injured, I would rush out to defend *your* honor. But then that would be only fitting, considering your high birth. But you, my lord, are better known for your gentleness than your jousting. Why, it is often said that you more closely resemble your sweet mother than you do your bold father."

Sir Gawain, being a true gentleman and knight, did not reply to Sir Kay's taunts. "I do not think," he said quietly, "that anyone has ever seen me run from a sword. I am, as always, at your service, sir."

Sir Gawain rode out to meet the mysterious challenger, but he went unarmed. Courteously, he greeted the knight who had so rudely dispatched two of Arthur's court. The knight did not answer; indeed, he did not even turn to see who was approaching.

"Sir," Gawain continued, "since you refuse my greeting, does that mean you intend to meet me with force? Your skill is not in dispute, but you have insulted a king and his lady, and every knight at their disposal is eager to do battle against you. Why don't you just come and let me take you with me to the king? He is my uncle and will forgive you if I ask on your behalf. I promise you will not lose any honor if you do."

Again, the mysterious knight made no answer. Sir Gawain was not easily discouraged. He asked, he cajoled; at last, he even threatened, but the knight did not even turn his head to look at him. He acts as if he's lost his senses, Gawain thought. Suddenly he remembered an occasion when he had lost his own. He had given his heart in love and his senses had seemed to flee. Gawain rode around to the sorrel's head to see what the knight was staring at so fixedly in the snow. When he saw the three drops of blood, he threw his mantle down to cover them.

Parzival spoke then, but not to Gawain.

"My lady," he said, "do not leave me. Didn't I save you from Clamide and make you my wife? Didn't I give everything to save your people? Why do you hide yourself from me? And where"—he jerked his head up and looked about—"is my lance?"

"My lord," said Gawain gently, "your lance is yonder. Shattered in a joust."

"Hey there, sir. Do you mean to fight?" Parzival asked, seeing Gawain for the first time. "You'd best beware. I've knocked one or two men off their horses in my day."

"I have no wish to joust with you," Gawain answered. "There is encamped just over there a king and his lady with all his court. I wish to guide you to them. I promise no one will attack you if you come with me."

"Who are you, gentle knight, and who is your king?"

"I am the son of Lot and nephew to

cousin's curse, he had made amends both to the duchess and to the Lady Cunneware. He could almost forget Sigune's anger and the shame of Wild Mountain as every knight and lady drank to his good health and praised his skill and courage.

But his joy was not to last one single night.

"Son of Uther Pendragon!" A shrill voice pierced the merriment of the feast like a lance through a shield. The whole company turned to see, on the edge of the circle, a huge mule, saddled and bridled like the most noble of horses. Its rider, too, was dressed in a beautiful robe with a peacock hat, but the face under the hat made them all shrink back in repulsion. It was a woman, but what woman would want to claim her for a sister? Her black plait falling down her shoulder was as coarse as pig's bristles. Her nose jutted out like a dog's and her teeth were like the tusks of a wild boar. Her skin was like

King Arthur, who is encamped here. Perhaps you have heard of me as well. My name is Gawain."

"Ah, yes, Sir Gawain," Parzival replied. "They shall not credit me with special honor for being received kindly by you. It is well known that you receive everyone with kindness. And still I thank you, but I cannot go to Arthur's court. I was there once before and on my account a lady suffered humiliation. Arthur's steward beat her as though he were felling a tree. Until I can make amends for that, I will not appear before the king."

Gawain laughed despite himself. "You have paid that account in full," he said. "The steward lies now in Arthur's tent with a broken arm and a broken leg. He was your second conquest of the morning. Sir Segramors, who is no mean fighter either, is in his own tent nursing a wounded pride. Now come with me, good sir, and give your greeting to our gracious king and his lady."

Parzival could not bring himself to speak to the kindly Gawain of his cousin's curse or the shame of Wild Mountain. He took off his helmet and followed as he was bid.

As Gawain and Parzival approached the camp, the Lady Cunneware saw them come. Even though his face was still filthy from rust and perspiration, she recognized Parzival. "You have sent three knights, one of whom was my own brother, to protect me, and today you yourself have made amends for that unjust beating the steward gave me," she said as she greeted him. She kissed his grimy cheek and ordered her serving boys to see that he was bathed and provided with rich clothing.

When Arthur heard who the strange visitor was, he was delighted. He ordered the meadow in the midst of the camp to be cleared of snow in the shape of a great circle, so it would seem that his knights and their ladies were feasting at a giant

Round Table. That night, Parziv[al] seated at a place of honor and all (e[xcept] perhaps Sir Kay) rejoiced that the h[and]some Parzival had returned. Even Q[ueen] Guenever forgave him for the deat[h of] Ither, for, if the truth be told, there w[ere] few ladies in Arthur's court who had n[ot] felt a fondness for that bold knight wh[o] had died so shameful a death—pierce[d] by a javelin in the hand of an untutore[d] boy. Duke Orilus begged forgiveness for the sins he and his brother Lahelin had committed against the kingdoms that belonged to Parzival and pledged full restitution.

Parzival was glad to pardon all who asked, even King Clamide, who had wronged his wife. He had no appetite for revenge that night when he saw how graciously they all received him.

Indeed, Parzival's heart was lighter than it had been since the day he rode out from Queen Condwiramurs's castle. Despite hi[s]

wrinkled leather and her nails like the claws of a lion.

Even those who had never seen her before knew at once who she was— Cundrie, whom some called the Sorceress, but perhaps should rather call the Prophetess, for she had never been known to tell an untruth.

"I do not greet you as king, son of Pendragon," she said to Arthur, her voice grating as metal scraping against metal, "for you have allowed a malignancy into your circle. The Round Table is corrupted. Like a fruit with a worm in its heart, it will be destroyed from within. And you, son of Pendragon, have welcomed this worm into your bosom. I cannot greet you; you have lost all honor."

Before the astonished Arthur could reply to this strange salutation, Cundrie rode her mule into the circle and stood directly before Parzival. She stretched out her clawed finger toward his face. "You call yourself the son of Gahmuret," she said. "I would deny it except that I know that your pure mother was never false. Still, how are you his son? That man of honor. He has another son whom you would call an infidel—a son he had of a Moorish queen. Yet that son, infidel though he may be, is as noble as Gahmuret before him. While you, you—you have earned Hell eternally," she cried. "May it begin for you here on earth. You were taken to Wild Mountain so that you might release that wretched king. Where was your compassion, son of Gahmuret and Herzoloyde? How could you fail to ask the question that would give Anfortas peace at last? You saw the bloody lance, the silver knives, the Grail itself, and yet you failed to ask. Woe, that I should be the one to say that matchless Herzoloyde's son has so fallen from the height of Heaven's honor to the lowest shame of Hell."

Cundrie began to wring her monstrous hands in despair and weep so that great tears crisscrossed her hideous features. "Alas, Wild Mountain, that you have lost all hope of consolation." With that, Cundrie left Arthur's circle and disappeared into the shadows of the forest.

There was no more feasting that night. The joy of Arthur's court vanished like the moon behind dense clouds. Parzival took leave of his friends. When Clamide asked him to plead with the Lady Cunneware on his behalf, he did so, and perhaps it was a little comfort to Parzival to know that Cunneware would have a noble husband to protect her now.

He himself sought out the king. "What the Lady Cundrie has said is true," he said. "Although it was not my intention to cause harm. Perhaps I took the good Gurnemanz's teaching too much to heart. Many will mock me for a fool, I fear, and I blame no one who despises me. For my part, I must leave your company. Somehow I must find the Grail again. That is my only aim now, to go once more to Wild Mountain. To this quest I will devote my life to the very end of my days."

They all sorrowed to see him go. Lady Cunneware had her own pages dress him and bind his armor. She was grateful to him, not only for her restored honor but for a royal husband. "May God preserve you on your way," she said.

"God?" Parzival answered. "What is God? If God were all-powerful, none of this terrible misfortune would have happened. Today I quit his service. Let him be angry with me if he will."

And with those terrible words, the wretched Parzival rode forth alone.

King Arthur, who is encamped here. Perhaps you have heard of me as well. My name is Gawain."

"Ah, yes, Sir Gawain," Parzival replied. "They shall not credit me with special honor for being received kindly by you. It is well known that you receive everyone with kindness. And still I thank you, but I cannot go to Arthur's court. I was there once before and on my account a lady suffered humiliation. Arthur's steward beat her as though he were felling a tree. Until I can make amends for that, I will not appear before the king."

Gawain laughed despite himself. "You have paid that account in full," he said. "The steward lies now in Arthur's tent with a broken arm and a broken leg. He was your second conquest of the morning. Sir Segramors, who is no mean fighter either, is in his own tent nursing a wounded pride. Now come with me, good sir, and give your greeting to our gracious king and his lady."

Parzival could not bring himself to speak to the kindly Gawain of his cousin's curse or the shame of Wild Mountain. He took off his helmet and followed as he was bid.

As Gawain and Parzival approached the camp, the Lady Cunneware saw them come. Even though his face was still filthy from rust and perspiration, she recognized Parzival. "You have sent three knights, one of whom was my own brother, to protect me, and today you yourself have made amends for that unjust beating the steward gave me," she said as she greeted him. She kissed his grimy cheek and ordered her serving boys to see that he was bathed and provided with rich clothing.

When Arthur heard who the strange visitor was, he was delighted. He ordered the meadow in the midst of the camp to be cleared of snow in the shape of a great circle, so it would seem that his knights and their ladies were feasting at a giant

Round Table. That night, Parzival was seated at a place of honor and all (except perhaps Sir Kay) rejoiced that the handsome Parzival had returned. Even Queen Guenever forgave him for the death of Ither, for, if the truth be told, there were few ladies in Arthur's court who had not felt a fondness for that bold knight who had died so shameful a death—pierced by a javelin in the hand of an untutored boy. Duke Orilus begged forgiveness for the sins he and his brother Lahelin had committed against the kingdoms that belonged to Parzival and pledged full restitution.

Parzival was glad to pardon all who asked, even King Clamide, who had wronged his wife. He had no appetite for revenge that night when he saw how graciously they all received him.

Indeed, Parzival's heart was lighter than it had been since the day he rode out from Queen Condwiramurs's castle. Despite his cousin's curse, he had made amends both to the duchess and to the Lady Cunneware. He could almost forget Sigune's anger and the shame of Wild Mountain as every knight and lady drank to his good health and praised his skill and courage.

But his joy was not to last one single night.

"Son of Uther Pendragon!" A shrill voice pierced the merriment of the feast like a lance through a shield. The whole company turned to see, on the edge of the circle, a huge mule, saddled and bridled like the most noble of horses. Its rider, too, was dressed in a beautiful robe with a peacock hat, but the face under the hat made them all shrink back in repulsion. It was a woman, but what woman would want to claim her for a sister? Her black plait falling down her shoulder was as coarse as pig's bristles. Her nose jutted out like a dog's and her teeth were like the tusks of a wild boar. Her skin was like

# five

## The Lost Knight

**VER** thousands of dreary miles, Parzival rode and rode, this way and that, across the world. Whether on the sorrel's back or on a ship borne forward by wind and waves, he saw nothing to cheer him. When challenged, he raised his lance or drew his sword, but why mention those savorless struggles as though they had been adventures? There was no honor for him now in conquest. He never knew defeat. He must not. He did not care for his life. That was of little worth to him now. He fought only to rid his trail of an obstruction, dogged as

an ancient wolf on the scent of its last quarry. This one thing I will track down; then lay me down upon the earth to die.

Four years and more he roamed the world, his bones aching with weariness, his heart sick with longing, his soul heavy with despair. Searching, searching, his eyes strained in searching for a castle that would not let itself be found.

He did not know the year or the day or even whether it was night or day when he came upon a tiny house, more like a cell, freshly built in the wilderness through which he rode. There was a light at its one small window, which drew him toward it. Perhaps, he thought dully, I should ask directions, for, as usual, he had no notion of where he was.

"Is anyone there?" he called.

"Yes."

Hearing a woman's voice, Parzival dismounted, tethered the sorrel to a nearby tree, and unbound his sword. Then he went to the window.

Inside he saw a woman at what seemed to be her prayers. When she saw him there, she rose from her knees and came to meet him at the window grate. She was dressed like one who has given her life to God, but on the hand that carried her Psalter, Parzival saw a ring with a sparkling gemstone, not the kind of ring a woman sworn to poverty would wear. He must be careful, he thought; this woman is not what she appears to be.

As he stared through the bars of the window into the cell, he saw no cooking pots or utensils, nor was there any garden where food might be grown.

"Madam," he asked, "how is it you can live here alone in the wilderness?"

"You need not worry about my food. Every Saturday, Cundrie the Sorceress brings me food enough for a week from the table at Wild Mountain. Alas, if food were my only concern—"

At the mention of Wild Mountain, Parzival's long-dead heart gave a shudder. The lady went on: "I see, sir, that you stare at my ring. It was given to me by the knight I was pledged to marry, but to my eternal grief, he was killed before we were wed. In God's eyes, nonetheless, I am his bride and will be so forever. That is why I continue to wear his ring. He body lies below that very spot where you espied me on my knees in prayer."

When Parzival heard this, he realized that the grief-aged woman in the cell was his cousin, Sigune. He took off his helmet, and she recognized him as well.

"You are Parzival," she said. "Well, Cousin, how has it fared for you? Do you know by now the meaning of the Grail?"

"I have found nothing but unhappiness in that quest," he said. "Cousin, if you knew how much I have suffered. I have been parted from my wife, who is more to me than life. I have lost honor with my fellows. Do not go too hard on me."

"I no longer think of you as my enemy," Sigune said gently. "It is plain to see how much you have lost by failing to ask wretched Anfortas the question."

"God himself was against me," Parzival said. "Or I would have fared other than I did. But tell me how it goes with you. My burden is so heavy, I will not even feel it if you lay yours upon me as well."

"Dear Cousin," Sigune said. "I pray that God, who is the source of all comfort, will comfort you." To this Parzival did not answer. Sigune continued, "Would it be possible, I wonder, to follow a track to Wild Mountain and thus find your way there once again? Cundrie the Sorceress was here not long ago. The track of her mule is still fresh in the underbrush, if you follow it—"

Parzival took hasty leave of Sigune,

mounted the sorrel, and found the hoofprints of Cundrie's enormous mule. He
followed them through the woods along
a narrow path that wound high above a
deep chasm. Perhaps—his heart was now
full wakened in his breast—perhaps today
he would find that cursed castle—

"Halt there!" A knight was barring the
path. "Who are you who dares beat a track
through my lord's forest?" he cried out.
"Don't you know that you court mortal
danger when you come too close to Wild
Mountain?" The knight was fully armed
and rode a great black warhorse. From the
turtledoves embossed on his shield, it was
clear that he had come from the castle itself.

There was no room on the path for a
proper joust, but the knight came charging
toward him nonetheless. They struck
lance upon lance and backed and charged
and struck again until in one final charge,

Parzival knocked the castle knight off his horse into the chasm. But in the lunge, Parzival could not hold the sorrel back, and it plunged off the path as well. As horse and rider fell into the chasm, Parzival grabbed the branch of a tree and hung there, watching helplessly as his beloved red sorrel rolled and crashed against the scrub and through the underbrush, to break its neck at last on the rocks in the bottom of the crevasse. Meantime, the castle knight clambered up the opposite bank, headed, no doubt, for the safety of Wild Mountain and the comforts of the Grail.

Sorrow upon sorrow. Now his only companion was dead and he no nearer the end of his quest than before. Slowly and painfully, Parzival climbed up the slope to the path, and there, waiting for him, its reins dangling down as though in invitation, was the great black warhorse from

Wild Mountain. Parzival swung up into the saddle. He had lost his lance, his sorrel, his hope, but he clung to the powerful flanks of the warhorse, and in the rhythmic stride and proud head he found a true friend for many a year to come.

Wild Mountain itself was not to be found. Another winter came. He and the warhorse slept close together, each body saving the other from a freezing death. Food was scarce for man and beast and hope more meager yet. The sun rose, the sun set, but there was no counting of the days. The world seemed a cold and endless wilderness. A man might ride forever and never come out into the sunlight or into sight of a great castle that refused to show its face.

So it was that on one of these nameless days, Parzival was riding to nowhere. There was a light snowfall and Parzival in his cold armor sat shivering in the saddle.

He saw coming toward him through the woods a gray-bearded man, followed by his wife and two young daughters. They were dressed in sackcloth and their feet, despite the weather, were bare.

Parzival greeted the family with due courtesy, for their bearing was noble if not their attire. The old man greeted him in return, but with a rebuke. "I see, sir, that you are a knight. Why is it then that you do not observe this holy season? Why, in God's Holy Name, do you ride armed, when you should, indeed, be walking barefoot?"

"There was a time," Parzival answered, "that I knew the name of one called God. I even vowed him my service. But in return, this God gave me nothing but sorrow. So I do not look for help from that source anymore."

"Do we speak of the same God?" the pilgrim asked. "Do you mean the one who came to earth born of a virgin? Do you mean he who died for our sins upon the dreadful cross on this very day? Do you mean the God who gave his life that all might live?"

Parzival did not answer.

"Follow us," the pilgrim said gently. "There is a holy man not far from here. To him you can confess your misdeeds, and he will help you find forgiveness."

The daughters were, to tell the truth, more interested in Parzival's handsome face than in his sins. They persuaded their father that they should share their food with the knight and urged their parents to find a place where the poor fellow might warm himself. But Parzival thought, It will not do for me to go with these good folk. I no longer serve the God to whom they are devoted. So he thanked the pilgrims for their kindness and went on his unknown way.

Now, though, his mind was churning and his frozen heart began to break up like river ice in the thaw of spring. He recalled from his distant childhood echoes of his mother's teaching and began to wonder. Who was it hung the stars and spread out the earth? Was it indeed the one called God? If such a one was powerful enough to create all things, might he not be able to grant comfort to a sorrowing soul? "Oh, God, if you can help," Parzival cried out to the dark forest, "if you can help, then help me now."

There was no answer from the silent trees, but in the stillness, Parzival felt a tiny stir of hope. "If," he said to himself, "if God is so great, then he has the power to guide both man and beast. If he wishes to help me, he will guide my horse to find such help. Now," he said, throwing the reins over the horse's ears, "go. Go where God chooses." With that he spurred his horse into a gallop.

Within minutes, the warhorse of Wild Mountain had borne him to the mouth of a cave where there dwelt a holy man, a hermit named Trevrizent. When the good man heard Parzival's greeting, he came out. "Sir," he said at once, "has some desperate encounter forced you into armor on this holy Good Friday? Dismount, if you will."

Parzival did so. Then he told the hermit how his horse had brought him there and added, "Sir, if you can, guide me. For I am a sinner."

"Tether your horse to yonder tree; then come in with me, for I can see that you are bitter cold."

How good it felt to take off that icy steel and warm his limbs before the fire. There was no wine or meat or bread in that cave, but kindness makes a feast.

When Parzival was warmed, the hermit said, "Tell me, my son, why have you come to me?"

"There was a time," Parzival said, "when my life was full of joy. I vowed to a cave where there dwelt a holy man, a hermit named Trevrizent. When the good man heard Parzival's greeting, he came out. "Sir," he said at once, "has some desperate encounter forced you into armor on this holy Good Friday? Dismount, if you will."

Parzival did so. Then he told the hermit how his horse had brought him there and added, "Sir, if you can, guide me. For I am a sinner."

"Tether your horse to yonder tree; then come in with me, for I can see that you are bitter cold."

How good it felt to take off that icy steel and warm his limbs before the fire. There was no wine or meat or bread in that cave, but kindness makes a feast.

When Parzival was warmed, the hermit said, "Tell me, my son, why have you come to me?"

"There was a time," Parzival said, "when my life was full of joy. I vowed to

He saw coming toward him through the woods a gray-bearded man, followed by his wife and two young daughters. They were dressed in sackcloth and their feet, despite the weather, were bare.

Parzival greeted the family with due courtesy, for their bearing was noble if not their attire. The old man greeted him in return, but with a rebuke. "I see, sir, that you are a knight. Why is it then that you do not observe this holy season? Why, in God's Holy Name, do you ride armed, when you should, indeed, be walking barefoot?"

"There was a time," Parzival answered, "that I knew the name of one called God. I even vowed him my service. But in return, this God gave me nothing but sorrow. So I do not look for help from that source anymore."

"Do we speak of the same God?" the pilgrim asked. "Do you mean the one who came to earth born of a virgin? Do you mean he who died for our sins upon the dreadful cross on this very day? Do you mean the God who gave his life that all might live?"

Parzival did not answer.

"Follow us," the pilgrim said gently. "There is a holy man not far from here. To him you can confess your misdeeds, and he will help you find forgiveness."

The daughters were, to tell the truth, more interested in Parzival's handsome face than in his sins. They persuaded their father that they should share their food with the knight and urged their parents to find a place where the poor fellow might warm himself. But Parzival thought, It will not do for me to go with these good folk. I no longer serve the God to whom they are devoted. So he thanked the pilgrims for their kindness and went on his unknown way.

Now, though, his mind was churning and his frozen heart began to break up like river ice in the thaw of spring. He reca[lled] from his distant childhood echoes of [his] mother's teaching and began to wonde[r,] Who was it hung the stars and spread out the earth? Was it indeed the one called God? If such a one was powerful enough to create all things, might he not be able to grant comfort to a sorrowing soul? "Oh, God, if you can help," Parzival cried out to the dark forest, "if you can help, then help me now."

There was no answer from the silent trees, but in the stillness, Parzival felt a tiny stir of hope. "If," he said to himself, "if God is so great, then he has the power to guide both man and beast. If he wishes to help me, he will guide my horse to find such help. Now," he said, throwing the reins over the horse's ears, "go. Go where God chooses." With that he spurred his horse into a gallop.

Within minutes, the warhorse of Wild Mountain had borne him to the mouth of

serve one called God, but he is the grandfather of all my troubles. It is said that
God will help, but where was his help
for me? He has given me nothing but sorrow." In his anger, Parzival stood up. He
began to pace back and forth before the
hermit's fire.

The hermit sighed. "First, sit you down,"
he said. "I would that you could trust God,
for he can help us both. He it is that both
made the world and saves it by his grace.
The angel Lucifer rebelled against God,
and then, again, the first man that he
made. But God is lover yet of all, and will,
I know, be your true help. First, my son,
tell me why you have such anger against
him."

"My greatest sorrow is for the Grail,"
Parzival said. "And then for my wife. I
long for them both."

"It is fitting that a man should long for
his wife," the hermit said, "but it alarms
me that you long for the Grail. That is

arrogance itself. Don't you know that no man approaches the Grail of his own will, but only he that the Grail bids to come? I know this because with these eyes I have seen that holy thing."

"You were there in the presence of the Grail?" Parzival asked.

"I was," the hermit replied, but Parzival could not bring himself to say that he, too, had seen the Grail.

"I do not boast," the hermit continued, "for it was not by my deserving that I saw the Grail but by God's grace. Guard against pride, my son." Trevrizent stirred the embers so that they danced up. He seemed not to see the pain in Parzival's eyes. "I shall tell you an unhappy tale of pride. There is a king called Anfortas, whose pride has brought him to the most terrible agony. In his youth, he pursued vain honor and the admiration of pretty ladies. These things are not in accord with the Grail. Now he lies there at Wild

Mountain guarded by the knights of the Grail, who do not let anyone enter there, except"—and here the hermit sighed—"one callow youth, and for him it would have been better if he had never come. He failed to ask about the king's wound and so rode away bound in sin."

He turned now to look Parzival in the face. "But I digress. Anfortas was son and heir to that castle, but he was not content to follow the direction of the Grail. One of the castle knights had met his death in a joust and lost his armor and warhorse thereby to a knight named Lahelin." His eyes narrowed. "Your name is not Lahelin, is it? I ask because I saw on your horse's saddle the sign of the turtledove, which is the emblem of the knights of Wild Mountain."

"No," Parzival answered. "I am the son of a man who died in battle. I beg you remember him in your prayers. His name was Gahmuret. I am not Lahelin. I never stripped a corpse but once, when I was a green youth who knew no better. I should confess this crime to you. I slew Sir Ither, the Red Knight, with a javelin, and when he was stretched out dead, I took from him his armor, his weapons, and his horse."

"Then you are Parzival," the hermit said. "Alas, poor nephew, you have sinned more than you know, for you are blood kin to Ither, whose blood you have shed. And more than that, my dear sister Herzoloyde has died for sorrow that you left her side."

"Don't tell me that!" Parzival cried. "If you are my uncle, tell me in truth. Tell me that I have not killed both my cousin and my mother."

"I cannot lie," the holy man said. "You broke my sister's heart when you left. Another sister, the mother to that unfortunate Sigune, died at her daughter's birth. Our youngest and last remaining sister serves as mistress in Wild Mountain, where my poor brother is king but has no joy in that title.

"Your grandfather, King Frimutel, died when we were young, and my brother Anfortas became his heir. But when the first bristles appeared on his cheek, he sought out many loves and bold adventure, careless of the life that must be lived by one who is protector of the Grail.

"A heathen king approached, determined to win the Grail for himself, and Anfortas, arrayed in pride, rode out to joust with him. The heathen king was slain, but my brother carried back to Wild Mountain the point of that infidel's lance and part of the shaft, buried in his side. He was so pale, we thought that he would surely die, but the physician probed deep into that wound until he drew out both lance point and bamboo shaft. In gratitude, I gave up all knightly honor on that day and gave myself to God.

" 'Who will be protector of the Grail?' they asked, for my brother's wound had festered. But I did not believe that God would let him die. We carried him into the presence of the Grail, and indeed, he did not die. But his continued life proved affliction greater than death would ever be.

"We sent to every part of the world for herbs and balms and antidotes, but there was nothing found that could ease his pain. At last, we fell down before the Grail and on our knees asked for some sign that his agony would have an end. We were directed to a certain ancient writing. A knight would come, it said, and ask the question, and all our sorrows would be ended. But no one, man, woman, or child, was to prompt the knight. He must ask the question out of his own compassion or else it would prove harmful to the king, causing him pain more terrible than before. If the knight should fail to ask the question, then so would fail his power to heal.

But if he should ask the question, then that same knight would become king and all sorrow would cease. Anfortas would be healed, but he would be king no more."

For a long time, the hermit was silent. But Parzival could not speak.

"We waited," the hermit continued, "for the coming of this good knight. We nursed my poor brother's wound as best we could, though nothing eased the pain. At times, the stench from the wound grew so terrible that we would carry him down to the lake so that the wind would carry away the odor. Those who saw him there thought he had come to fish. It was from this that people came to call him the Angler.

"After several years, I left Wild Mountain and came to this place to pray that the knight would hasten. My prayer was heard. A knight did come. The one I told you of earlier. Would to God that he had left my prayer unanswered. This knight was led to the castle, he saw my brother in his agony, but he did not ask the question. He left in shame."

The hermit got to his feet. "Enough of these sad tales," he said. "We must find nourishment for you and your poor horse. It is too bad that snow lies so late upon the ground. I have none of the fodder of Wild Mountain to offer, nor its rich foods. We shall have to gather bracken and yew tips to feed your mount and dig roots for our own supper."

After prayers, they ate the humble supper the hermit had prepared. "Nephew," he said. "Pray do not despise this food."

"I have never tasted better," Parzival answered.

They went out to where the horse was tied. The good man stroked his nose. "I apologize, my friend," he said to the horse, "for your poor meal. If you were at home in Wild Mountain where you belong, you would be feasting now."

At this, Parzival could hold back his secret no longer. "Dear Uncle, I have come to you in my extremity and you have received me with all kindness. Please, I beg you, do not cast me out now, or I will be completely without hope. I swear to you that I was wholly without evil intent, but that man who rode to Wild Mountain, who saw the Grail and the sorrow, and who still asked no question—I was that man."

The hermit was unable to contain his grief. "What are you saying? Where were the five senses God gave you? How could you be in the presence of Anfortas's agony and not cry out in compassion?"

Parzival covered his face and began to weep. "There is no hope for me. I have killed kinsman and mother and failed the quest ordained by God. I curse the day my mother brought me into the light!"

"Do not despair, my son," the hermit said gently, laying his hand on Parzival's shoulder. "Though every human voice should curse you and every human heart harden itself against you, the mercy of God knows no bounds. God himself will not abandon you."

Then Trevrizent drew the grieving Parzival back into the cave and gently urged him to do penitence for his wrongdoing and to put his trust once more in God, who creates and saves.

"But still, Nephew," he said, "you have not told me how you came to be riding a horse from Wild Mountain. I pray that upon your other sins you have not stolen something that belongs to the Grail."

So Parzival told him about the joust with the knight from Wild Mountain.

"You did not kill a knight from that castle!"

"No, Uncle, I saw him safely away, but my own poor horse lay dead and this war-horse I won by fair battle."

His uncle was content. For a week or

more, Parzival stayed there with Trevrizent, learning more of the mercy of God and the depths of his love. He was happy to share the roots and herbs that the hermit ate. He still did not know the way to Wild Mountain when he rode forth from that holy cave, but his heart was cleansed and full of hope.

# Six

## The Grail King

**ARZIVAL** did not know as he rode forth so hopefully from Trevrizent's cave that the greatest battle of his life lay just ahead. An infidel king, whose ships lay at anchor in a nearby port, was riding out alone, bent on adventure. When he saw Parzival approach, the infidel raised his lance in challenge. This time, Parzival was not mooning over drops of blood on the snow. He saw the strangely appareled knight at the same moment as he was seen. The two of them spurred their mounts forward and charged.

The infidel was amazed. Never had a

knight kept his saddle under such a charge. Both knights renewed the attack, galloping toward each other again and again and again until the mouths of their great warhorses were afoam and both beasts too weary to continue.

The two warriors leapt from their saddles. It was Ither's sword that Parzival drew from its sheath. He had left the sword from Wild Mountain with Trevrizent, for it seemed too heavy a burden to bear.

The infidel matched him blow for blow. Both helmets were badly dented. Both knights could feel warm blood flow beneath the cold steel of their armor.

At last, with one mighty stroke, Parzival brought Ither's sword crashing down upon the infidel's helmet. The blow toppled his opponent to the ground, but Ither's sword broke off at the hilt. The blade went flying off into the underbrush.

The infidel jumped to his feet, his sword

still in his hand. Parzival steeled himself against one last fatal blow. It did not come. Instead, his enemy spoke: "I vow. You are the kind of man who would keep fighting without a weapon. But how could I gain honor from such a victory? If we stop fighting now, you will lose no honor, for I swear if your sword had not broken, you would have made chopped meat of me. I propose a truce—at least until we can catch our breath and rest our bones."

The weary Parzival nodded, and both men sat down against a grassy mound. The infidel spoke first. "Who are you, bold knight? It is not hard to guess that you come from noble parentage."

When Parzival hesitated, the stranger went on. "No," he said. "I have been discourteous. I will not force you to reveal yourself. But let me introduce myself to you. I am Feirefiz Angevin, king of many lands, but they are far from here."

"You cannot be called Angevin!" Parzival said. "I am Angevin, heir through my father of Anjou." As he spoke, he remembered something Cundrie the Sorceress had said that terrible day when she had cursed him in the presence of Arthur's court. "Still, there is one other who might call himself Angevin. He lives in heathen lands, but he may be my brother. Sir," said Parzival, rising to his feet, "if you would take off that helmet and let me see you, I could tell if you might be he. Don't fear, I shall not attack you unhelmeted."

The infidel laughed and stood up. "You could hardly attack me at all without a sword, unless you mean to wrestle. That would hardly be a fair fight, as, on your first hold"—he pointed his sword at the buckle on Parzival's breastplate—"I could take my sword and part you flesh from sinew. Here," he said, hurling his sword far into the bushes, "now we are even. Tell me about this infidel brother of yours."

Parzival told the strange knight what

Cundrie had said. "So," he concluded, "he is neither black as a Moor nor white as an Angevin. He must rather be pied, a mixture of black and white, though I'm not sure how that can be."

Again Feirefiz laughed. But then he took off his helmet, and, indeed, he was neither wholly white nor black, but something between the two. When Parzival saw that the strange knight was truly his brother, he took off his own helmet and embraced him.

Feirefiz was overjoyed. "Take me to see our father," he said. "All my life I have longed to see his face."

"I, too," said Parzival, "but, alas, he died before I was born. But come, I will take you to Arthur's court. There you will meet kinsfolk aplenty."

When Sir Gawain heard that Parzival and a stranger were riding for the place where Arthur's court was presently encamped, he rode out with joy to meet them. He greeted them both and took them to his own tent so they might bathe off the grime and rust of battle, and he gave them fresh garments to wear.

Again, the king ordered a feast where Parzival and his new-met brother would be the guests of honor. Feirefiz was deeply touched by the king's warm hospitality. He sent word to his ships that gold and jewels should be brought. These he distributed to everyone, so that even the strolling entertainers left that place rich as nobles.

In the midst of the feasting, a horse and rider appeared. The rider was a woman dressed in rich black samite. Her robe was decorated with a flock of turtledoves embroidered in fine gold thread. No one could see her face because it was covered by a heavy black veil.

She rode into the middle of the circle to

where King Arthur and his queen were seated. She greeted them both. "Son of Pendragon," she said. "I have come to beg forgiveness for a great wrong that I have done to one of your noble guests."

Immediately, she turned to Parzival, who sat beside the queen. She climbed off her great black horse and fell on her knees before him. "Son of Gahmuret," she said. "For the sake of your good mother, grant me pardon for the wrong I have done you." Parzival realized then that the woman was Cundrie the Sorceress.

"Your curse has given me much pain," he said. "But the sin was mine alone. I bear you no malice."

"Oh, happy man!" Cundrie cried out, and when she stood, everyone could see that it was she. "God is about to show his grace through you. You are destined to be the Grail King. Already God's mercy is at work. Your wife, Condwiramurs, had twin sons soon after you left her. They are now lusty lads—five years old. Kardeiz shall one day rule over Anjou and Waleis and Norgals, which are yours by birth, but as for Lohengrin, he shall be your heir at Wild Mountain.

"Now, my lord, choose one companion whom you trust with all your heart and follow me. For I am sent to lead you into the presence of the Grail."

With joy, Parzival asked his brother Feirefiz to go with him, and as soon as they could make themselves ready, the Lady Cundrie led the two sons of Gahmuret to the castle of the Grail.

There was no joy at Wild Mountain. It was the time of year when Anfortas knew the severest pain. He longed for death; indeed, he would have died, except that his people brought into his chamber the Grail, whose dreadful power kept the wretched king alive.

"If you had any love for me," Anfortas

groaned, "you would not bring it near me. You would leave me free to die. What good am I to you? I can no longer rule, for I myself am nothing more than slave to this most grievous pain. Pray, let me die."

Still they would not remove the Grail. "If you do not let me die," the king cried out, "I will stand before the throne on the Day of Judgement and curse you all before Almighty God."

His people were sorely tempted to release him, but they clung to that faint hope, once dashed, that a deliverer would come. So even as he cried and railed against them, they daily brought in the Grail and forced the king to live against his will.

They were not pitiless. They nursed him as tenderly as they could, anointing him with precious oils and rubbing his body with powders ground from the horns of exotic beasts. They brought in spices and burned incense from distant lands, seeking to cleanse the noxious airs that rose from the king's gangrenous wound.

But the king could only curse their ministrations, and all, all was sorrow in that dread place.

And then one morning, as the guards of Wild Mountain rode out to patrol the forests of the Land of Wildness, they spied the Lady Cundrie accompanied by two knights. A shout rang out and sounded and resounded through the forest.

Feirefiz was alarmed as an armed troop of men on black horses appeared to block their way and he urged his brother to the attack, but Cundrie caught his reins. "They are the Knight Templars of Wild Mountain," she said, "come to escort us."

When Parzival and Feirefiz reached the courtyard of the castle, they were offered baths and fresh garments, but Parzival would not wait. He took off only his helmet. "Lead me to the king," he said.

At the great door, he hesitated, for there, propped against his pillows, lay Anfortas, shivering beneath his furs. Burning incense could not hide the stench that permeated the air. The king looked across the hall to where Parzival stood, but he did not seem to recognize his nephew. His face was so drawn and contorted with pain that it looked to Parzival as one carved onto a crucifix. Poor, wretched man. Why did no one come to his aid?

Tears sprang to Parzival's eyes and he cried out, running as fast as his heavy armor would allow. He fell on his knees beside the king. "Dear Uncle," he said, through his sobs, "what is wrong with you?"

"God be praised," the king said. "You have come at last."

The Grail Knight had come. He had in his compassion asked the question, and King

Anfortas was healed. But as the writing foretold, Anfortas was no longer king. Gladly, he gave his crown to Parzival and became one of the Templars whose life was devoted to the Grail. Feirefiz, too, rose to great honor. He married Anfortas's sister Repanse de Schoye, the very maiden who had been deemed worthy to bear the Grail in her own hands.

But before these things happened, the two of them went forth, Parzival and Feirefiz together, to meet Queen Condwiramurs and her twin sons. The reunion between Parzival and his lady was, for all its tears, so joyful that it cannot be told here with any justice. Just say that the brave and compassionate pair grew wiser and more loving with every passing year and that their praise was sung in many distant lands.

This is not the end. There are many stories left to tell—of Feirefiz, the Noble Infidel; of kindly Gawain; of his fellow knights and their beloved king. Young Lohengrin himself went forth one day from Wild Mountain, bearing the secret of the Grail. But that, too, is another story, to be told another day.

# About This Legend

**SOMETIME** in the latter part of the twelfth century, there was born to a Bavarian family of the lesser nobility a son who was destined to become one of the greatest German medieval poets. Wolfram von Eschenbach became a knight, serving a number of feudal lords, and then, during the early part of the thirteenth century (probably between 1200 and 1210), this knight who claimed that he was illiterate wrote a 25,000-line epic poem that has endured for nearly eight hundred years.

Where Wolfram got the idea for *Parzival* is a matter that scholars argue. Wolfram says that he did not get it from the French poet Chrétien de Troyes, who wrote a poem around 1180 titled *Perceval*, which was quite famous at the time. Scholars disagree, pointing to similarities between the two epics. Wolfram says he heard the story from someone called Kyot, but since there is no evidence that such a person ever existed, Kyot may well be a product of Wolfram's very fertile imagination. His claim of illiteracy probably meant that he did not know Latin or Greek and was, therefore, not a scholar. It is evident that he used as the basis of his poem stories about the Holy Grail in wide circulation at the time, but Wolfram clothed the well-known legend with both humor and a profound seriousness that no other medieval writer quite matched.

Wolfram's Parzival is in some senses the Percival of the more familiar English tales of the Round Table. He is the boy raised in the wilderness, ignorant of chivalry and the great King Arthur. But in Wolfram's tale, he is much more than that. He is the innocent fool who through trial, loss of faith, suffering, repentance, and at last, redemption, becomes the Grail Knight he was destined to be.

In this retelling, I have simplified Wolfram's long poem, leaving out the chapters that tell of his father Gahmuret's adventures and those of his friend, Sir Gawain. I have also left out Wolfram's explanation of why he wrote the poem and his commentary on life. Some of this is fun to read and shows the poet's delightful sense of humor. If you want to read the whole poem as Wolfram wrote it, there is an English translation by A. T. Hatto. It is Professor Hatto's translation (*Parzival* by Wolfram von Eschenbach, Penguin Classics, 1980) on which this retelling is based.

Why, you may wonder, is it necessary to have yet another story of the Holy Grail? Because Wolfram, I believe, tells the story as no one else has told it. Professor Hatto points to Wolfram's unique vision in his introduction: "At one point in his poem Wolfram humourously wonders how it is possible for so impecunious a knight as himself to describe such wealth and luxury as he unfolds. We, in our turn, wonder . . . how it was possible for a knight of such humble station and education to enshrine in his poetry an understanding of the Christian message deeper and truer than that of all the popes and most of the saints of his day."

# About the Author

KATHERINE PATERSON's books have received wide acclaim and been published in twenty-two languages. Among her many literary honors are two Newbery Medals, for *Bridge to Terabithia* and *Jacob Have I Loved*, and two National Book Awards. Her latest book, *Jip, His Story*, received the Scott O'Dell Award for Historical Fiction. Ms. Paterson has long been interested in the legend of Parzival and used it as the basis of her novel *Park's Quest*.

The author lives in Barre, Vermont, with her husband. The Patersons have four grown children and three grandchildren.